DAVE KEANE

Joe Sherlock

KID DETECTIVE

Case #000004:
The Headless Mummy

HarperCollinsPublishers

JOE SHERLOCK, KID DETECTIVE MYSTERIES

Case #000001: The Haunted Toolshed

Case #000002: The Neighborhood Stink

Case #000003: The Missing Monkey-Eye Diamond

Joe Sherlock, Kid Detective, Case #000004:
The Headless Mummy
Copyright © 2007 by David J. Keane
All rights reserved. Printed in the United States of America.
No part of this book may be used or reproduced in any manner
whatsoever without written permission except in the case of brief
quotations embodied in critical articles and reviews. For information
address HarperCollins Children's Books, a division of HarperCollins
Publishers, 1350 Avenue of the Americas, New York, NY 10019.
www.harpercollinschildrens.com

Library of Congress Cataloging-in-Publication Data is available.
ISBN-10: 0-06-076193-8 (trade bdg.)
ISBN-13: 978-0-06-076193-6 (trade bdg.)
ISBN-10: 0-06-076192-x (pbk.)
ISBN-13: 978-0-06-076192-9 (pbk.)

Typography by Christopher Stengel
1 2 3 4 5 6 7 8 9 10
❖
First Edition

For Mom and Dad, who blessed me with a marketable sense of humor

—D.K.

Contents

• Chapter One •
Nightmare on Baker Street

My fourth case as a private detective arrives while I'm having a nightmare.

Not a good sign of things to come.

This nightmare starts out as many of my bad dreams do—with a cricket stuck in my nose. They call this kind of dream a recurring dream, which means you dream it all the time. And for some strange reason, I always dream about crickets crawling up my nostrils.

Sounds weird, I know. But it gets worse.

As I flop around, trying to snort the insect out of my nose, the floor suddenly turns into a sea of ants. I start to sink into the ants like quicksand.

It keeps getting worse: Suddenly I'm not wearing pants.

Then I hear my little sister's voice.

"Not that ridiculous grasshopper dream again," Hailey says, slapping me on my forehead like she's playing a game of Whack-a-Mole.

I am so startled by my sudden return to the real world that I fall off the edge of my bed. I proceed to slap myself

all over to knock off any leftover imaginary ants.

"Ants, too?" she chuckles. "Sherlock, you are so messed up."

"Thanks for waking me up," I say simply.

"Doreen heard you screaming," she explains.

"Who the heck is Doreen?" I ask. It's at this point that I notice the surgical glove she's holding. It's filled with water and tied off at the wrist. Hailey has painted a face on it with big red lips and long eyelashes. "And you think I'm weird?" I whisper.

"Say hello to Doreen," Hailey says in the kind of voice people use when they talk to babies. "She's our long-lost sister." Hailey tickles the glove on the chin.

Maybe my nightmare hasn't ended after all.

I wait a moment for my head to clear. "That's just a plastic glove filled with water."

"Sherlock!" she says, pretending to be angry. "Look what you've done; you're making our baby sister cry."

"She probably just sprang a leak," I say. Hailey is supposed to be my assistant, but she's actually more like a monkey wrench dropped into my brain's delicate gears.

Hailey rocks Doreen in her arms and hands me a slip of folded paper.

"What's this?" I ask.

"Mr. Klopper from down the street dropped it off while you were napping," she says with a shrug. "He said it's very urgent."

"Why didn't you wake me up?" I ask,

GIRL CHAT SLEEPOVER

4

jumping to my feet. "I wasn't napping, you know. I just fell asleep."

"There's a differ-ence?"

"Yes!" I snap. "A nap is something you do on purpose. I fell asleep by accident."

"Oh, brother," Hailey says, waving at me like I'm being silly. "Besides, Doreen says you need to catch up on your beauty sleep."

I hold my breath as I unfold the paper. I know before I even read Mr. Klopper's note that the painfully long and boring wait for my next case has finally ended.

I'm immediately struck by three things as I read Mr. Klopper's note:

1. He sure knows how to get to the point.
2. He likes to doodle.
3. Hailey is reading over my shoulder.

"Do you mind?" I sniff without bothering to look back at her. "I can't concentrate with people reading over my shoulder."

She giggles. "Let's be honest, you can

never concentrate. Do you want me to read it to you?"

"I can read!" I grumble, looking over my shoulder to give her some of my best stink-eye. "I'm just trying to figure out if Mr. Klopper's doodles are part of the mystery."

"Those aren't doodles," Hailey sighs. I could swear I hear her eyes rolling in her head. "That's early Egyptian writing. It's some sort of message."

"I already know that," I say, although I'm really thinking that I'm not even that great at reading English, let alone scribbly ancient languages.

"That's called Egyptian hieroglyphics," Hailey says slowly and clearly, as if my brain has turned into a fruitcake. "It's an ancient form of writing. Each of those symbols is called a glyph and has a special meaning."

"Do you think I was born yesterday?" I ask

with a squeak in my voice. I secretly clench my teeth at the sheer humiliation of having a little sister who's smarter than I am.

"No, I can't tell you what those symbols mean," she says, anticipating my next question, which is just one of her many irritating habits.

"Oh, you're not fluid?" I scoff, as if she's not so smart after all.

"You mean 'fluent,'" she corrects me.

"That's what I said," I say with another unconvincing squeak.

"No, I can't translate that," she explains. "I went through a big Egyptian phase when I was younger, but it's not like I can read it."

"Younger?" I snort.

"Hailey, you're only in the second grade."

I'm reminded of the time my teacher, Miss Piffle, asked me how I could have a little sister with a brain  like a power plant, while my brain works more like an old hamster running on a rusty exercise wheel.

"You're done with your nap?"

It's my mom. She's poked her head through my open door.

"It wasn't a nap," I say. "I fell asleep by accident."

"There's a difference?" she asks.

"Did you two have a meeting to coordinate your attack?" I ask.

My mom shakes her head in confusion. "All I know is that Mr. Klopper is here again."

"He is?" Hailey and I chirp at the same time.

"Does he still have a good head on his shoulders?" Hailey asks.

"He's waiting in the family room . . . with Billy Frick and Jessie."

"Oh, no," I croak. "I've got to get him out of there before Jessie and her creepy boyfriend scare him away for good."

As I hurry down the hallway, I'm struck by the fact that the great Sherlock Holmes never had to deal with a big sister who could creep out his clients so bad that they'd go running for their lives. There isn't a moment to lose! I'm not about to let my fourth client slip away, whether or not I can read his Egyptian doodles.

• Chapter Three •
Long Beard

MR. KLOPPER   BIG SHEEP

When you first lay eyes on Mr. Klopper, all you see is his beard. It's a whopper. A force of nature. It's easily the biggest, puffiest beard on the planet. It basically looks like he's walking around with a large sheep stuck to his neck.

"Mr. Klopper, sorry to keep you waiting," I say with a sigh of relief, mostly because he hasn't left yet but also because his head still seems securely attached to his body.

"Sherlock Sherlock," he says, apparently thinking my first name is the same as my last name. He's not the first. It's a pretty common mistake. See, everybody has called me Sherlock for so long that most of the residents of Baker Street have forgotten that I actually have a first name. But I don't mind. Joe just doesn't seem to stick to me, kind of like a spitball without enough moisture. But Sherlock has more than enough sticky mouth goop—which is how I like it.

"How can I help?" I say, shaking Mr. Klopper's meaty hand.

I may not know how to read body language, but he sure seems uneasy. The way his eyes keep darting over to Jessie and Billy Frick tells me that he'd rather discuss his situation in private.

"Why don't we step into the living room?"

I ask, and extend my arm in a slick "you go first" kind of way. He doesn't pick up on my slickness, so I add, "After you, of course." Mr. Klopper takes the bait; he and his beard exit stage left.

Jessie and Billy Frick seem to be unaware of the drama going on right in front of them. In fact, whenever Billy comes over, Jessie seems like she got hit on the head with a grand piano. She smiles, giggles, and snorts like aliens have invaded her body and are taking it out for a test drive.

By the time I reach the living room, I find Mr. Klopper sitting quietly across from Hailey. He's staring uncomfortably at Doreen, who's sitting up alertly on the couch, like she can't wait to hear what's going on.

"It's okay, Mr. Klopper," I say. "Whatever you need to say to me, you can feel safe saying in front of Doreen." This statement seems to irritate Hailey, which I consider a small victory.

After several awkward moments, Mr. Klopper pulls his eyes away from the glove. "I'll be off to jail if you can't help me extricate myself from this predicament," Mr. Klopper announces, stroking his beard like it was a cat.

I have no idea what

half of those words mean.

Hailey saves me. "That means he's in a serious jam, Sherlock."

"Yes, I know what it means," I say, although everybody in the room knows that I don't. I'm a terrible liar. But I can solve mysteries like most people can crack eggs, which is why the people of Baker Street come to my door when they're in a pinch. "Please, tell me everything," I say, borrowing one of the phrases I've learned from watching hundreds of Sherlock Holmes movies.

I don't know that the story he's about to tell me will take me to places where The Great Detective wouldn't go in four thousand years.

"I've lost the head of a four-thousand-year-old mummy," Mr. Klopper says, cutting right to the chase.

I wait for him to add more, but he seems choked up. "Interesting," I say, although I'm really thinking that the idea of some ancient guy's head bouncing around in somebody's trunk like a coconut makes my stomach roll over.

"I work at the private Egyptian museum in town," he continues. "Tonight is our big annual fund-raising gala. This party is the only time we open our doors to the public. During the festivities, we unveil our newest showpiece to important community leaders, scientists, reporters, and bigwigs from other museums."

"'Bigwigs'?" I ask.

"Yes, other museum muckety-mucks," Mr. Klopper says.

"'Muckety-mucks'?" I ask, feeling slightly embarrassed now.

"Yes, the big fish," he says, looking puzzled.

Now I'm really lost. "'Big fish'?"

Mr. Klopper looks over at Hailey, then back at me. He shifts uncomfortably on the

BIG FISH?

couch. "Why do you keep repeating everything I say?"

"Sherlock, he's talking about important people," Hailey says. "Excuse my brother, Mr. Klopper. He sometimes gets lost in those little empty spaces between words."

"Oh, I see," he says, fluffing up his enormous beard with his stubby fingers. To be honest, Mr. Klopper's beard is distracting me. It seems to be sprinkled with tiny crumbs, bacon bits, and mysterious white flakes that keep getting flung into the air every time he touches the thing. The sight of it is making my stomach do jumping jacks.

MYSTERIOUS BEARD JUNK!

"That mummy's head needs to be in place when our museum director pulls the sheet off the display case at seven-thirty this evening. It's a priceless artifact that I . . ."

"Did someone steal the head?" I ask.

"I did," he says.

"What?" Hailey and I blurt out at the same time. Doreen remains silent.

"I borrowed it, actually," he says, nervously dragging his fingers through his beard and filling the room with more air pollution. "I secretly brought it home last night to take some photographs of it. I snuck it back into the museum this morning. But when I tried to return the head to its proper place, it was suddenly gone."

The room goes silent. I clear my throat.

"Gone?"

"The mummy's head had turned into a head of butter lettuce," he mumbles.

"How could some old guy's pickled head turn into a head of butter lettuce?" I ask.

"I have no idea," he says, his voice rising. "It's so strange. It's as if I'm being punished for doing something I shouldn't have done. Nobody knows I took the head, but they'll figure it out soon enough. I'll be shipped off to prison. That head is priceless."

Wow! This case is a doozy. But something doesn't add up. "Are you sure nobody knows you took the head?" I ask.

"As far as I know, you two are the only people who know of this," he says with a sniff.

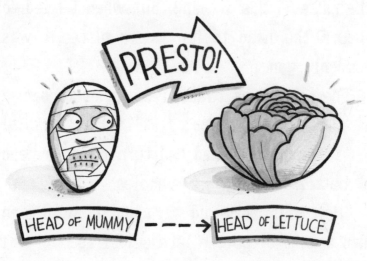

HEAD OF MUMMY ---> HEAD OF LETTUCE

"But it will not take long for the museum director to figure out it was me. Will you help me, Sherlock Sherlock?"

"All I can do is try," I say. My natural mystery-solving instincts have already started to stretch their hamstrings. "When was the last time you saw the head?"

"Last night in my basement," Mr. Klopper says in a faraway voice. "I took some digital photos. I'm thinking of writing a book about mummies, and I—" His voice tightens up with emotion. "This may be the result of some kind of ancient mummy curse," he whispers.

I get chills on the back of my neck. I spring to my feet and smack off any leftover imaginary ants that may be crawling around back there. Mr. Klopper also jumps to his feet and looks at me like I've lost my mind.

I begin to explain my fees, but Mr. Klopper doesn't seem to be listening. I tell him I'll meet him at his house in five minutes. He exits noiselessly.

"You're going to need help on this one, big brother," Hailey says. Or maybe it was Doreen. I can't be certain. I'm already "in the zone" from a mental standpoint, which is the place a detective needs to be when the stakes are this high.

Chapter Five

Dead Heads on Parade

"How much would a mummy's head weigh?" I ask over my shoulder.

My head is still swimming in the strangeness of this case as I hustle down Baker Street with Hailey trailing behind me. She's singing lullabies to Doreen, who she refuses to leave behind. Hailey tells me you don't leave family behind. I know she doesn't really believe we're actually related to a rubber glove, but she continues the whole business because she knows it's driving me loco.

"It wouldn't weigh much," Hailey says cheerfully. "They used to remove the brain while they were preparing the body to become a mummy."

"What?" I ask, stopping dead in my tracks. "Why would they do that?"

"They were preparing the body for the trip to the afterlife," she says casually.

"That makes no sense," I say, holding my stomach. "It's hard enough to find a clean pair of socks with a whole brain; how were those guys supposed to find the afterlife with a hollow skull?" I shake my head in disbelief. "Did they remove the head from the body to get the brain out?"

"No, that wasn't how they removed the brain," she says thoughtfully. "The brain was usually pulled out through the nose with a long, bronze hook—"

"STOP!" I holler. My lower back suddenly gets sweaty. My legs go watery. My tongue feels too big for my mouth. It's maddening, but I always get dizzy and light-headed when it comes to anything of a medical nature. In fact, just the thought of cotton balls or one of those wooden tongue sticks can make me instantly queasy.

Hailey usually finds my dizzy spells

hilarious. Sensing her opportunity to toss a few more medical bombs my way, she continues. "Most of the major organs were pulled out, too. They were each put in separate jars called—"

"You know what?" I shout to drown out her voice. "I don't need to know every bit of mummy-making trivia to solve this case. Is that clear?" I inch closer to some nearby bushes to soften my landing in case I actually pass out. The world is doing cartwheels around me.

"They did leave the heart in, though."

"HAILEY!"

"Touchy!" she says. She places Doreen on her shoulder and starts patting her back like she needs to burp. "I'm just trying to have a little fun."

I place my sweaty palms on my knees and take a few deep breaths. "Mr. Klopper's in big trouble," I say between clenched teeth. "So you can at least pretend to be interested in helping him."

"You're scaring the baby," she says.

"Maybe she just has an air bubble," I grumble. I run my fingers through my hair. "Remind me to have my head examined once this is over. I think my brain has been removed, too, considering I invited you along to solve a mystery."

"I think you might be right," she says, although I'm not really listening anymore. I'm too busy staggering past the final two houses before I turn into Mr. Klopper's driveway.

"I'm up here!" Mr. Klopper hisses. I turn and see his beard in an upstairs window. "I'll be right down. Don't say anything to Lorraine." The beard vanishes.

"Who the heck is Lorraine?" I ask, turning to Hailey. "Is there another glove I haven't met yet?"

"Lorraine is Mrs. Klopper's first name," Hailey says. "She's a librarian and a good friend of mine. You'd better watch out, Sherlock; she doesn't suffer fools lightly."

"What's that supposed—" Before I can

finish, the Kloppers' door swings open and my eyes take in the figure of Lorraine Klopper. Thankfully she doesn't have a massive beard. But she is holding the ugliest, scariest hairless monkey that I have ever seen.

"So you must be Sherlock, the kid detective," Mrs. Klopper says with a hint of amusement in her eyes. "I've heard about you."

"What is that?" I squawk, unable to peel my eyes off the creature she's holding.

"Oh, Doreen, let's say hello to Fluffy!" Hailey squeals, and runs up to the bug-eyed beast.

"Fluffy?" I croak.

Hailey even touches it. Gross! For a moment, I think the animal may be a weasel that someone has cruelly attacked with an electric shaver.

"This is our cat," Mrs. Klopper chuckles, probably noticing my lip curling up in disgust. "She's a Sphynx. It's a hairless breed."

"I thought so," I manage to blurt out.

Hands down, Fluffy the nude cat is the freakiest, most unnatural-looking pet on planet Earth. It doesn't even have whiskers, for pete's sake! Who ever heard of a hairless cat? Why not get a toothless beaver? Or a three-legged snake? Or a goldfish that doesn't know how to swim?

I'm feeling sweaty again.

"The Sphynx is a

FLUFFY THE "CAT"

THREE-LEGGED SNAKE!

recent breed of cat," Hailey says, rubbing the unfluffy Fluffy behind her hairless ears. "The first was born in Canada about forty years ago. They're very special cats."

"That's my girl," Mrs. Klopper says to Hailey, like she couldn't be prouder. I think she even winks at her.

I figure that Mrs. Klopper must know Hailey from Minds of Tomorrow, a group of nerds that Hailey belongs to. Basically, Minds of Tomorrow is a small collection of overly smart kids who meet at the Baskerville main library on Saturday mornings. As far as I can tell, they just sit around flipping through books while complaining about how hard life is

Because we can...

when your brain is as big as a watermelon.

I can see that Mr. Klopper is now nervously fidgeting with his beard behind Mrs. Klopper and the hairless wonder. I'm struck by the fact that Mr. Klopper and Fluffy are at opposite ends of the hair spectrum.

"Sherlock Sherlock," Mr. Klopper says urgently from behind his wife. "Why don't I show you that scarab I was telling you about?"

Scarab? What in the world is he talking about?

"Would you like to pet her before you see

the scarab?" Mrs. Klopper says with a twinkle in her eye.

Trying not to seem like I'm about to yark the entire contents of my digestive system down Fluffy's enormous ears, I run my fingers over the beast's back. It purrs like a hairless motor. I can feel its delicate bones. It feels like a leather hot-water bottle. I may as well have scraped my fingernails across a chalkboard! I have the willies so bad that, for an instant, I seriously consider pulling a finger off Doreen so I can wash my hands.

"Why don't we go have some tea in the garden?" Mrs. Klopper says to Hailey.

I can't get away

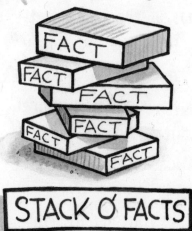

STACK O' FACTS

from Lorraine and the naked cat fast enough. I hurry after Mr. Klopper and follow his bouncing beard down the stairs to his basement. Could this case get any weirder? From sheep-sized beards and water-filled gloves to brainless skulls and cats plucked as smooth as chickens, the strangeness just keeps coming.

I recall something Sherlock Holmes tells his assistant, Dr. Watson, in one of his movies: Facts are like the mud that you make bricks out of. And you can't solve a case without any bricks. So someone better start slinging mud fast!

Sadly, this nugget of wisdom doesn't give me any comfort, because when I step into Mr. Klopper's basement, I feel like I've been hit with a ton of bricks.

SUPER SPONGE CAKE VISION!

SOAKING UP A CRIME SCENE?

My eyes sweep over Mr. Klopper's basement and soak up every detail like two tiny sponge cakes. But two words tumble around inside my head like a pair of acrobatic hippos: "Dead End."

Dang! I know The Great Detective would never jump to this conclusion. But sometimes my ability to solve mysteries relies more on instinct than logic.

In case you don't already know, instincts are

the things we do without actually needing to think about them. Blinking, yawning, and picking our noses are simple examples that everyone can understand. But sometimes they're more complicated. And while I can never say exactly where my instincts come from, they're usually right on target. I've learned to listen to them.

My hero, Sherlock Holmes, almost never uses instincts to solve his mysteries. Instead, he relies on pure logic and an amazing ability to tell you some guy's complete life story from the way his boot left a scuff mark on a windowsill.

"Jeepers" is all I can think to say as I take in Mr. Klopper's basement. I had been expecting a dark, moist dungeon with stacks of books, messy piles of research papers, discarded mummy parts, and half-eaten apples lying all over the place—a place where it would be easy to lose your head. But this basement is more like a museum. It's spotless, organized, and bright.

"Where did you keep the head while it was here?" I ask, creeping myself out just asking the question.

"I photographed the artifact here," Mr. Klopper says, indicating a small digital camera on a stand.

"Then where'd it go?" I ask.

"I left it here on my worktable until the next morning," he says.

I'm struck by something that doesn't make sense. "How does Lorraine—I mean, Mrs. Klopper—feel about you plopping old guys' heads down all over the place?"

"Honestly, she can't even stand to hear me talk about my museum work anymore," he says

glumly, slumping onto a stool near the camera. "She says I've become obsessed with Egyptian artifacts. She tells me I've become distant, a shadow of my former self. But even so, I'd never leave a four-thousand-year-old treasure just lying around."

"So it was in some kind of airtight artifact case or something like that?" I ask, trying to move things along.

"No, it was in a Taste Safari animal crackers box."

"Are you kidding me?" I gasp. "Why on earth would you carry something so valuable around in a box that was designed for little vanilla lions, tigers, and bears? Oh, my!"

"It was actually one of the assorted flavor

boxes, with chocolate, cherry, boysenberry, and—"

"Mr. Klopper!" I interrupt. "I need facts if I'm going to get you out of this. But some facts don't help me make bricks, they just get my wheels stuck in the mud. So please stick to the point."

"I used the animal crackers box to sneak out the head," he says, nervously shooting out another spray of beard pollution. "It was the only way I could get it out without anybody noticing."

The gears in my head have become gummed up with the desperation of this situation. I let out a heavy sigh of exasperation. I have the sinking feeling that Mr. Klopper's turkey is cooked.

"I was down here most of

the night, photographing it," Mr. Klopper starts up again all on his own. "In the morning, I came down here, snatched the box off my worktable, and left for work. At work, it sat on my desk all morning. I thought I'd have a chance to get the head back to its proper place when everyone was out for lunch. But when I opened the box, it had turned into a head of butter lettuce."

"What a mess," I say with a shake of my head. "Could the head have rolled out of the box somewhere in the car?" I ask hopefully.

"No, I could feel it in the box when I carried it into work, past Benito. He's our museum's security guard."

The head of butter lettuce is the thing that doesn't

make sense. It simply doesn't fit. Then I have an idea. "Was the animal crackers box ever alone on your desk? Did you ever leave it unattended this morning?"

Mr. Klopper looks up and blinks a few times, quietly recalling the dreadful events of this morning. "Of course I did. I had several staff meetings about preparations for tonight's event. But nobody knew it was there! Besides, who would do such—"

"I must get inside your museum right away!" I announce, my heart galloping into high gear. "I need to see your desk. Your office. Where you work. Mr. Klopper, I think this is an inside job."

"It will be difficult to—"

"It will not be as difficult as going to jail," I say, instantly feeling bad about my outburst. I can actually see Mr. Klopper's beard lose some of its puffiness. "There's no time to discuss it. We must leave immediately."

"I must warn you," Mr. Klopper says with a slight tremble in his voice. "Our museum is extremely private about its operations. I will have to sneak you in. And if you're caught by Benito or the museum director, I may not be able to protect you."

"I eat risk for breakfast," I peep, thinking instantly that it's a dumb thing to say, especially considering my ultrasensitive stomach.

• Chapter Eight •
Some Other Time

"Could someone please explain to me how this old guy's head got detached from the rest of him in the first place?"

Hailey, Doreen, and I are holding on for dear life in the backseat of Mr. Klopper's car. Mr. Klopper is driving his car like he just robbed a bank. It's funny, but you never think of people with giant beards as fast drivers.

"Back in the eighteenth century," Mr.

Klopper says, "visitors to Egypt liked to bring home souvenirs of their vacation down the Nile River. So they often snapped off hands, toes, and heads of mummies as keepsakes."

As if the crazy driving isn't enough to make my stomach feel like it's about to blow peach cobbler all over the back of Mr. Klopper's getaway car, the thought of cracking off some guy's toe and stuffing it in my pocket is speeding the process along nicely.

Thankfully, Mr. Klopper stomps on the brakes as he decides at the last moment that running through a red light is not worth it.

My stomach breathes a momentary sigh of relief.

Of course, Hailey just *has* to add her two cents. "Mummy hands were the most popular thing to take, because they often had fine jewelry and valuable amulets wrapped inside."

"Very good," Mr. Klopper says, looking admiringly at Hailey in the rearview mirror.

"Mr. Klopper, do you always drive this fast?" I ask.

"I've taken much too long for lunch," he says tightly. "I don't want to raise any more suspicion. Benito, our security guard, doesn't seem to like me too much."

I think for a moment about what he means by that last sentence but decide to let it go.

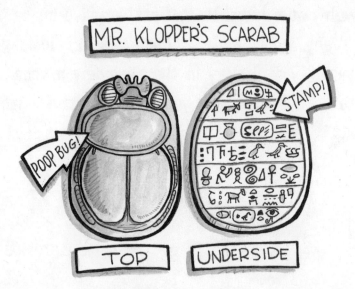

MR. KLOPPER'S SCARAB

POOP BUG!

STAMP!

TOP   UNDERSIDE

Instead, I look down at the clay scarab Mr. Klopper gave me back at the house—so I wouldn't look like an idiot if Mrs. Klopper asked me about it.

"Scarab," I have just learned, is the name for a chubby black beetle that the Egyptians just went nuts over. They made lots of these little beetles because they saw this bug as a magical symbol of new life.

"The scarab is a dung beetle," Hailey says,

48

noticing me studying the beetle.

"'Dung'?"

"That means poop," she says, enjoying showing off. "Scarabs lay their eggs in animal droppings. When the eggs hatch, dozens of baby beetles come bursting out of each poop ball. It was seen as magical."

I quickly roll down my window.

Between Mr. Klopper's driving and stories of magical poop bugs, it's a miracle I haven't already launched a stomach rocket.

Thankfully, we hit another red light.

I study the scarab while we wait. Apparently it was once used as some sort of stamp because it has lots of Egyptian writing on the back—which brings to mind Mr. Klopper's original note to me.

"Mr. Klopper, you haven't said anything about the symbols you wrote on your note to me," I say, just as the tires squeal in protest when Mr. Klopper hits the gas again. "What do they mean?"

"They don't mean anything," he says, looking back at me longer than I think he should, considering he's driving so fast we might actually travel in time. "Those were the same symbols scratched onto a slip of paper pinned to the head of lettuce. Very puzzling. It's just garbled nonsense."

"Weird," Hailey says.

"Weird," I murmur.

Doreen doesn't say anything, but I'll bet she's thinking the same thing.

Before I can ask a follow-up question, Mr. Klopper whips the car to the curb in front of what looks like a rarely used doorway at the rear of the museum. It doesn't even have a doorknob.

"Quickly," he says, "get out here and wait by this door. I will open it after I enter the building through the front entrance."

Before I know it, Hailey and I are standing on the sidewalk, watching Mr. Klopper's car roar away.

"Weird," Hailey says again in the sudden stillness.

"I'm sure it's about to get a whole lot weirder," I mumble.

• Chapter Nine •
Calling All Cars

SPYING DEVICE!

"**W**here'd you get the cell phone?"

Hailey is punching numbers into a cell phone that has somehow appeared in her hand. Speeding cars blow by us every few seconds. It seems like all of the drivers give us odd looks, as if they've never seen two suspicious-looking kids hanging around on the sidewalk outside a museum's emergency exit door.

"It's Mom's phone," Hailey explains, holding

it to her ear. "She gave it to me before we left. I told her I'd let her know what's going on."

"Mom has you spying on me?" I ask in disbelief.

"Relax," Hailey says, waving at me like I'm a pesky fly. "Mom should know where we are. She still thinks we're at Mr. Klopper's house."

"Mom never lets *me* take her cell phone," I protest.

"That's because you're always losing things," she says. "And besides— Oh, hi, Mom!" she says cheerfully, and turns away from me.

Where the heck is Mr. Klopper? Why is it taking him so long to open this door? And why do my cases always feel like poorly run fire drills?

I keep thinking about this last point. In his

movies, Sherlock Holmes spends his cases sitting by the fire for hours, reading the paper, sucking on a pipe, and bossing around his assistant. In the real world, things just don't work that way. Not only does your assistant rarely do what you ask, but working a real case feels more like riding a bucking bronco that's been covered with that artificial butter flavoring they squirt on movie popcorn.

I notice Hailey approaching me. She has closed the cell phone, but she looks terrible, as if she's just received some horrible news. My stomach drops. "What is it?" I ask breathlessly. "Is Mom okay?"

"Where is Doreen?" she asks in a faraway voice.

"I have no idea!" I say in a rush of relief and irritation. "You don't have it?"

"No, I don't have her," she whispers. She stares straight ahead

and blinks a few times, then hands me the phone. "I left Doreen in the back of Mr. Klopper's car. I must go find my baby!" Without another word, she runs past me in the direction that Mr. Klopper's car was headed just minutes earlier.

"HAILEY!" I shout after her. "It's just a stupid glove! We can make more Doreens later!"

She doesn't stop. She doesn't look back. She turns the corner and disappears.

My sister may be a member of Minds of Tomorrow, but she doesn't have a lick of common sense.

Just as I'm about to sprint after her, the emergency exit door bursts open with a loud groan. Mr. Klopper pokes his head out. "Hurry! Inside quickly!" he says, looking

around for Hailey. "Where is your sister?"

"Uh . . . uh . . . uh," I blabber, frozen to the sidewalk like a guy whose brain has just turned into Chinese chicken salad.

"Please, before someone sees us!" Mr. Klopper urges.

In half of a split second, I decide that Hailey can handle herself for now. I jump through the door and into an unlit hallway. In the darkness, I can barely see Mr. Klopper leading the way down the gloomy hall in front of me. Before the emergency exit door clicks back into place, I pluck the scarab stamp from my pocket and use it to keep the door from

closing. Thankfully, the heavy door doesn't crush the scarab into dust. The beetle only props open the door an inch, but it's big enough to keep the door from locking into place. Hailey can still get in!

As I wobble half blind down the hallway after Mr. Klopper's hurried footsteps, I feel as if I've once again been thrown head over heels from the buttery bronco's back.

Before I can take a half-dozen steps, I see Mr. Klopper's beard emerging from the darkness—it looks like a floating ghost! He's running. His breath sounds short and raspy. "You must hide!" he huffs urgently. "They're coming this way!"

• Chapter Ten •
The Closet Detective

I can't think of a single movie in which Sherlock Holmes was shoved into a broom closet. It's so dark in here, I can't hear myself think.

Even worse, I need to pee.

But as my Uncle Mycroft liked to say, it could be worse.

Now that I think about it, this was my uncle's most favorite thing to say. For

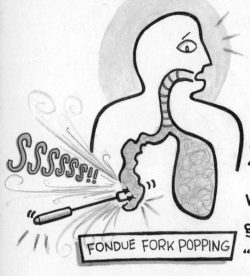
FONDUE FORK POPPING

example, if you just stubbed your pinky toe on the leg of a table, my Uncle Mycroft would say, "Hey, it could be worse." Then he'd give you an example: "You could have had your lung popped with the business end of a fondue fork." This was never helpful, but it did cut down on the complaining.

Getting shoved into a dark closet is surely a low point for any detective who takes his craft seriously. To make matters worse, it stinks of cleaning stuff, old mops, and stale vomit. And my bladder is starting to feel a lot like Doreen.

I guess I could start feeling my way around in the dark with my hands, but that barf smell has me spooked.

Then I remember the cell phone Hailey handed me outside.

I snatch it from my pocket and flip it open. The tiny, glowing screen lights up the room nicely. Yes, I'm in a broom closet.

But who should I call? I consider calling my mom, but she'd freak out. I think of calling a police officer I know named Lestrade, but I don't want to get the cops involved yet. So I call the next best thing.

"Lance?" I exclaim in surprise when my best friend in the world answers the phone on the first ring—his grandma always picks up!

"Hiya, Sherlock," he says with a glum sigh.

"What's wrong?" I ask.

"It's been a tough day," he says.

"Can you help me on a case? Hailey just—"

"I can't leave the house, Sherlock," he says grimly. "My grandma had to be rushed to the phrenologist."

"She's sick?" I instantly feel bad for calling. "Is that some sort of special doctor?"

"No," he says. "Her phrenologist is a lady who feels the lumps and bumps on my grandma's head to predict her future and give her advice."

"Dang it, Lance!" I exclaim louder than I should. "I thought she caught some disease. What happened to her palm reader?"

"They're not speaking," he says, his voice tightening. "I've never seen her this freaked out before."

I consider telling him that it could be worse but don't. "What happened?" I ask.

"She was in the kitchen this morning making me pancakes when all of a sudden she started screaming," he explains.

"Mouse?" I ask.

"I wish," he whispers. He's silent for a moment, working the words out in his head. "On the overcooked side of the second-to-last pancake . . . she can see the face of Don Chimpy."

"Who?" I ask, not believing what I'm hearing.

"Don Chimpy!" he scoffs, like I'm some kind of idiot. "He's the host of *Bug Chompers*, the most popular TV show in the country. Just imagine seeing your favorite TV host staring at you from the back of a pancake. She wrapped the pancake in foil and put it in the freezer and—"

"Lance!" I snap. "That's an amazing

DON CHIMPY

CHIMPY PANCAKE?

story, but I'm on a case right now, and I need help desperately! I've lost my sister. Mr. Klopper's lost his head. And I'm in a dark closet about to pee my pants. Are you saying I should call someone else?"

"I pulled it out of the freezer, and I just don't see Don Chimpy. To me it looks more like a seahorse with a wig on. Although if I hold it up to the light it—"

I snap the phone closed right in the middle of his sentence and return to complete darkness. I growl in frustration. *Why do I ever call him? I should have called—*

I hear footsteps coming down the hall. I hold my breath. The person out in the hallway has a flashlight that's sending light through the crack under the door. I can see my shoes.

The footsteps sound too quick to be Mr. Klopper's. They increase in speed as they pass the door in front of me. They stop. They shuffle around a bit. Whoever is out there must be near the back door that I came through. "What on earth!" a strange voice says sharply. Then I hear the back door snap shut with a bang. The footsteps hesitate and then go running past the door in front of me and down the hallway.

The poop beetle! I was using it to prop open the back door for Hailey, and now it's been taken. Dang it. This whole case is blowing up in my face—a lot like my last science project.

I clench my teeth. I need to take matters into my own hands or I'll never get this case solved. I take a deep breath, lower my chin, and grip the doorknob with a new determination to tackle this case head on, no matter what obstacles are thrown in my way.

The door is locked.

I shake, pound, and kick the door, but it will not open.

Holy corn dogs! What if Mr. Klopper gets arrested and forgets that I'm in here!

I can imagine the front page of next week's *Baskerville Daily News.*

Even my Uncle Mycroft would agree that things probably couldn't get any worse.

• Chapter Eleven •
Escape Plan

Sometimes you have to pee so bad, it becomes impossible to think about anything else.

But I try: Sailboats. French toast. Archery. Hairless cats and whether they cough up fur balls. Nothing works.

I use the glowing screen on my mom's cell phone to locate the nearest mop bucket in this closet in case I'm forced to take drastic measures.

The darkness gives me a moment to turn things over in my mind. I still hold on to the hope that I can crack this case before it's discovered that the mummy's head is missing and Mr. Klopper gets into serious legal trouble. My mystery-solving abilities rarely let me down.

I may not be in Minds of Tomorrow, but I'm smart in ways that are much harder to define. Sure, Hailey can rattle off pointless information, like the many uses of nitrogen gas and how to save someone who's choking on a fish bone. But all that book learning doesn't help her solve mysteries like I can.

And I'd do much better in school, too, if I wasn't so easily bored. In fact, my powers of concentration are similar to those of a small bird—just the sight of a shiny piece of foil or a twisted bit of kite string can wreck my entire train of thought. But I've never met a

mystery I couldn't
solve, which isn't a Santa Fe?
big help when your Hartford?
teacher is yelping at Augusta?
you to name the Honolulu?
capital of Delaware.

Detroit?
Dover?
Concord?
London?
Texas?

DELAWARE

Just then, without warning, the broom
closet door opens with a click.

My eyes can make out Hailey standing in
the hallway in front of me with Doreen in one
hand and her Girl Chat Sleepover pen-size
flashlight in the other. She blinds me with the
tiny beam.

"Why are you hiding in here like a dust
broom?" she whispers.

"I'm not hiding," I hiss. "I was locked in
here. In complete darkness."

"Why didn't you turn on the light?" she asks,
casually leaning into the closet and flicking a
light switch. The closet explodes with light.

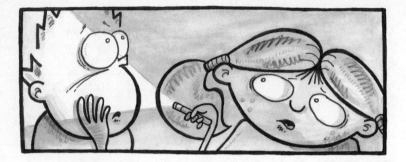

I'm speechless.

"C'mon," Hailey says, moving off down the hall. "Mr. Klopper says we have less than forty minutes before the gig is up."

"Wait!" I call out after her with some desperation. I snap off the light, shut the closet door, and stagger down the hall to catch up to her. "How did you get in? I propped the back door open with the scarab beetle Mr. Klopper gave me, but it was discovered."

"I know," she says. "I heard everybody talking about it. It's caused a big commotion. Everyone wants to know how it got taken out of storage and wedged into an emergency exit."

"Mr. Klopper stole that, too?" I gasp.

"I didn't think of that," she says. We stand silently for a minute. Doreen doesn't look worried.

"Mr. Klopper's been taking things home that he shouldn't have," I conclude with some certainty. "But I don't think he meant to steal any of this stuff. He doesn't seem like a bad guy, just someone who's used bad judgment."

"Well, that's your area of expertise," Hailey adds quietly.

I believe there's still a thin slice of hope remaining in the case's pie. "Well, at least the scarab mystery has probably bought us a little bit of time."

"Your diversion worked like a charm," she says with a snort, but I can't see the expression on her face in the dim light.

I hear excited voices somewhere in the building. "Hey, how did you get in here if the back door was closed?"

"Well, they're busy getting ready for a party with over three hundred guests," she says simply. "And someone's been swiping scarabs out of the storage space. It's nuts around here. So I just told the grumpy guard that I was the daughter of the lady bringing in all the trays of food. She's been carrying stuff in from a catering van parked outside the front entrance."

I have to admit, Hailey can sometimes be impressive.

"Why are you dancing?" Hailey asks in a near whisper.

I look down and realize that I am practically putting on a show. "Uh, I have to pee so bad I'm afraid to sneeze."

"I told you to go before we left the

house!" she hisses with irritation. "Your bladder must be the size of a chickpea. C'mon, the bathroom is this way." Her light bounces down the walls of the hallway.

"I can't walk that fast," I whimper.

Suddenly, her light snaps off. And before I know what's happening, I'm being pushed backward through a swinging door.

NORMAL BLADDER   CHICKPEA

• Chapter Twelve •
Sudden Death

UH-OH!

My first thought is that I'm covered in blood.

I can't tell for sure because the room Hailey and I have just tumbled into is so dark that I can't see the little sister right in front of my face.

"Could you get off me?" I wheeze.

"Gross!" she snarls quietly. "You're soaked!"

"Sorry, but I might be bleeding to death," I say, my throat closing up with emotion.

"Where's my flashlight?" she asks, seemingly unconcerned with my life-threatening injury. I can hear her hands slapping around on the cold, hard floor.

Then I have a thought that's even worse than my rapidly approaching death: "I may have just peed in my pants," I say in a sad and shaky voice.

"Oh, that has got to be a new low, even for you," she says, suddenly clicking on her flashlight and blinding me again. "Oh, no," she says in a strangely heavy voice.

"What?" I gasp. "It's blood? Hurry, go call an ambulance!"

"You're not bleeding!" she snaps. "And you didn't pee your pants! You popped Doreen!"

"Oh, what a relief," I say, snapping Doreen's remains out from under me.

"You killed our sister," she whispers. "How could you?"

"Would you stop with all your sill—" I stop myself midword when I hear voices right outside the door. Hailey turns off her light.

"I didn't want to say this in front of the staff," says the same gruff voice I heard near the emergency exit when the scarab was discovered. "But Klopper's been acting strange all day. I think he's our man. I should put him in the conference room and grill him like a sausage link."

"I was thinking the same thing, Benito," a woman says in an official-sounding voice. "Put Thomas in the conference room, but keep in mind that we've got half a

A KLOPPER SAUSAGE?

76

dozen visiting museum directors in this building at this very moment, and I don't trust any of them as far as I can throw them."

"Very good, ma'am," says Benito. I don't like the tone of his voice one bit. He sure sounds like he's out to get Mr. Klopper.

The footsteps fade away down the hall.

"I didn't even get to say good-bye," Hailey says, flicking her light back on. She holds up what's left of Doreen.

"It was a freak accident," I say.

"No, you're the freak!"

After overhearing the conversation in the hallway, I now know three things:

1. They haven't discovered that their mummy head has gone missing.

2. Mr. Klopper is already in trouble and may spill his beans if cornered.

3. All the guests in the museum may cloud the issue of who's responsible for using a delicate three-thousand-year-old scarab for a doorstop.

"Exploding under your big brother's butt has got to be the worst way to leave this world," Hailey says. "What a way to meet your end."

I shake my head. "I'm sorry about Doreen, but our chances of helping Mr. Klopper are fading fast."

"She was so young," Hailey sighs. "So full of hopes and dreams."

"Enough already!" I snap. "I'll buy you a whole box of disposable gloves when we get out of here. But Hailey, I'm going to pop worse than Doreen if we don't find a—"

"I'll wait outside," Hailey says quietly. She hits a switch before exiting through the swinging door, shedding light on the fact that I'm sitting on the floor of a bathroom.

With a mixture of disgust and horror, I realize that I'm in the girls' bathroom.

"Maybe my whole life has fallen under the curse of an ancient and very evil Egyptian curse," I say to nobody in particular.

GIRL CHAT
SLEEPOVER

"How do you know where Mr. Klopper's office is?" I ask.

"Minds of Tomorrow got a tour of this place," Hailey huffs, giving me her mad-dog eyes. She's still angry at me for popping our little sister. But I ignore her—right now we've got other fish to bake.

I must admit, now that I've used the bathroom I have a new bounce in my step, like

I'm two gallons lighter. "I thought this place was top secret," I whisper as we creep down a hallway. "I guess the kids in Nerds of Tomorrow get special privileges."

She doesn't answer. Unlike the dark hallway near the emergency exit, this part of the museum is brightly lit—perfect for catching two kids sneaking around. We turn left, run up some squeaky stairs, and turn right into an empty office with four desks.

I can tell which desk is my client's long before I see the THOMAS KLOPPER nameplate.

Three of the desks look like they were thrown here during a tornado. Mr. Klopper's desk, on the other hand, is shiny and spotless. Six finely sharpened pencils are lined up in perfectly straight lines. A pad of paper is positioned squarely underneath the pencils. In the middle of the desk stands a family-size box of Taste Safari animal crackers in assorted flavors.

Hoping for a miracle, I peek inside. No head. (Hey, you never know when your luck might change!) No head of lettuce, either. It's empty except for a slip of paper inside the box. I pluck it out.

The symbols that Mr. Klopper wrote on his message to me are written in pencil on one side of the paper. This must be the original note pinned to the lettuce. It has a slick film

FRONT

or coating on it. Its rectangular shape is irregular and crooked, which tells me that someone sloppily cut it out of a larger piece of paper. On the back the word "butt" appears on the right side.

"'Butt'?" I say.

"But what?" Hailey asks with a puzzled look on her face.

"No, not 'but,' but 'butt,'" I say.

Hailey considers me. "You may have internal injuries we can't see."

"Never mind," I say, and drop the note back in the box. Sure, it's a clue, but I have no clue what it means! Besides, how am I supposed to

BUTT

BACK

figure things out when I feel like I'm on some kind of wild goose chase—and I'm the one being chased by the wild goose?

I blow out a gust of air. "I don't get it," I say. "Mr. Klopper is so organized and neat, it's hard to imagine he could get himself into this mess."

Hailey shrugs. "He may be tidy, but he's been breaking museum rules—and maybe even several state and local laws—by sneaking stuff out of here."

"That's true," I say. "But usually people who lose things are careless."

"Mr. Klopper *is* careless," Hailey points out. "You've seen the way he drives. His wife told me he forgot all about their wedding anniversary, and he made the mistake of giving you a three-thousand-year-old Egyptian artifact."

"FOR THE LOVE OF RA!!!" booms an angry

and bodiless voice.

I let out a sound you'd normally expect from a prairie dog. I assume a crouching fighting stance.

"I AM CURSED!" the voice thunders from nowhere and everywhere at once.

"The headless mummy's spirit is here to get his brains back for his trip to the afterlife!" I blurt out.

Hailey remains motionless.

Staying in my best fighting stance, I walk sideways like a crab around Hailey to protect her from the angry Egyptian ghost. "Show yourself, great spirit of the headless mummy," I bellow like an idiot. I have to pee again. Dang!

Suddenly Mr. Klopper's desk chair rolls across the floor, as if being pulled by an invisible hand!

"The headless spirit wants to sit down and rest!" I peep, unable to take my eyes off the chair.

"I wish Doreen were here," Hailey says in a tiny voice.

a software program that rotates thirty different farm animals," she says cheerfully. "Cool, eh?"

I snap the phone open before the obnoxious rooster crows again. "Hello," I answer.

"Coach Lowney just called and wants to know why you're not at practice," my snarky big sister snarks on the other end of the line.

Oh, no! I'm on the Baskerville junior track team, and I keep missing practices for a variety of reasons—which I really don't have time to get into right now. "Could you just tell him I'm working on a case at the moment?" I plead into the phone.

"What am I? Your personal assistant?" Jessie snarls. "Call him yourself!"

If I ever made a list of all the things more irritating than my big sister, it would have nothing on it. "Let me guess," I snarl back, "your new husband, Billy Frick, had to go

"It's just me," Mr. Klopper says, crawling out from under his desk on his hands and knees.

"Y-you c-could have—you almost scared us to death," I stammer.

"What are you doing hiding under your desk?" Hailey asks.

"They're looking for me," he says, climbing to his feet and nervously flicking beard bits

in our direction. "I've clearly made a mess of everything. My whole life has taken a turn for the worse. Maybe I am obsessed, as Lorraine is always telling me. I think they know about the missing head. I should never have asked you children—"

"They only found the scarab you gave me!" I correct him. "We still have time to find your head."

"Oh, heavens, you were so scared you wet your pants!" cries Mr. Klopper, grabbing his forehead in panic.

"No, Doreen peed my pants!" I protest.

He just shakes his

head, not really listening anymore. "I'm afr we're all about to turn into pumpkins," says heavily.

As if this case couldn't get any weirder, rooster suddenly crows in my pants.

WHAT ON EARTH?

Wait! Hold the phone!

I pull out my mom's cell phone and stare a it. It cock-a-doodle-doos again in the palm my hand. My mouth falls open at the strange ness of it all.

"Uh, I've been downloading new ring tone for Mom," Hailey says with a goofy grin.

"And you chose a rooster?" I manage to ask before the phone crows another wake-up call.

"I actually installed

home and write a love song about your big ears."

The phone goes dead. She's hung up on me. Is it any surprise that the great Sherlock Holmes never carried a cell phone? I'm convinced they kill brain cells.

"Don't ask," I grumble when I notice Hailey and Mr. Klopper staring at me.

"I've got to get you kids out of here," Mr. Klopper begins again. "I don't want you to get in—"

"*MOOOOOO!*" the cell phone interrupts. This is unbelievable!

"Hey, I haven't heard the cow yet," Hailey chirps, clearly impressed by the farm animal phone.

"I HEAR SOMEONE UP THERE!" Benito roars from somewhere downstairs. "STAY WHERE YOU ARE!"

A herd of footsteps comes pounding up the

creaky stairs outside the office door. Our location has been given away by a cow!

"Quick! Down the back stairs!" Mr. Klopper says, racing to a door near the back of his office.

I shove the cell phone into my pocket. Then I grab the animal crackers box off his desk so as not to leave the evidence behind for Benito to find. I need to maintain Mr. Klopper's innocence for as long as I can.

The door is clearly labeled as a fire exit, and it wails in alarm when we throw it open. As we scramble down the dimly lit stairs, the cell phone moos loudly again.

If things could get any worse, I don't know how. But I'm sure I will soon find out. I'm on a roll!

• Chapter Fifteen •
Darkness Falls

"I'm not going down there!" I squeak.

A breathless Mr. Klopper unhooks a velvet rope that hangs in front of a stone stairway. The stairs plunge straight down into pure blackness. It looks like the slippery slope to the afterlife, the one that brainless mummy guys are always trying to find.

"There is no time to argue," Mr. Klopper gasps, grabbing a torch off the wall next to

• Chapter Fourteen •
Wake-up Call

"It's just me," Mr. Klopper says, crawling out from under his desk on his hands and knees.

"Y-you c-could have—you almost scared us to death," I stammer.

"What are you doing hiding under your desk?" Hailey asks.

"They're looking for me," he says, climbing to his feet and nervously flicking beard bits in our direction. "I've clearly made a mess of everything. My whole life has taken a turn for the worse. Maybe I am obsessed, as Lorraine is always telling me. I think they know about the missing head. I should never have asked you children—"

"They only found the scarab you gave me!" I correct him. "We still have time to find your head."

"Oh, heavens, you were so scared you wet your pants!" cries Mr. Klopper, grabbing his forehead in panic.

"No, Doreen peed my pants!" I protest.

He just shakes his

head, not really listening anymore. "I'm afraid we're all about to turn into pumpkins," he says heavily.

As if this case couldn't get any weirder, a rooster suddenly crows in my pants.

WHAT ON EARTH?

Wait! Hold the phone!

I pull out my mom's cell phone and stare at it. It cock-a-doodle-doos again in the palm of my hand. My mouth falls open at the strangeness of it all.

"Uh, I've been downloading new ring tones for Mom," Hailey says with a goofy grin.

"And you chose a rooster?" I manage to ask before the phone crows another wake-up call.

"I actually installed

a software program that rotates thirty different farm animals," she says cheerfully. "Cool, eh?"

I snap the phone open before the obnoxious rooster crows again. "Hello," I answer.

"Coach Lowney just called and wants to know why you're not at practice," my snarky big sister snarks on the other end of the line.

Oh, no! I'm on the Baskerville junior track team, and I keep missing practices for a variety of reasons—which I really don't have time to get into right now. "Could you just tell him I'm working on a case at the moment?" I plead into the phone.

"What am I? Your personal assistant?" Jessie snarls. "Call him yourself!"

If I ever made a list of all the things more irritating than my big sister, it would have nothing on it. "Let me guess," I snarl back, "your new husband, Billy Frick, had to go home and write a love song about your big ears."

The phone goes dead. She's hung up on me. Is it any surprise that the great Sherlock Holmes never carried a cell phone? I'm convinced they kill brain cells.

"Don't ask," I grumble when I notice Hailey and Mr. Klopper staring at me.

"I've got to get you kids out of here," Mr. Klopper begins again. "I don't want you to get in—"

"*MOOOOOO!*" the cell phone interrupts. This is unbelievable!

"Hey, I haven't heard the cow yet," Hailey chirps, clearly impressed by the farm animal phone.

"I HEAR SOMEONE UP THERE!" Benito roars from somewhere downstairs. "STAY WHERE YOU ARE!"

A herd of footsteps comes pounding up the

creaky stairs outside the office door. Our location has been given away by a cow!

"Quick! Down the back stairs!" Mr. Klopper says, racing to a door near the back of his office.

I shove the cell phone into my pocket. Then I grab the animal crackers box off his desk so as not to leave the evidence behind for Benito to find. I need to maintain Mr. Klopper's innocence for as long as I can.

The door is clearly labeled as a fire exit, and it wails in alarm when we throw it open. As we scramble down the dimly lit stairs, the cell phone moos loudly again.

If things could get any worse, I don't know how. But I'm sure I will soon find out. I'm on a roll!

• Chapter Fifteen •
Darkness Falls

"I'm not going down there!" I squeak.

A breathless Mr. Klopper unhooks a velvet rope that hangs in front of a stone stairway. The stairs plunge straight down into pure blackness. It looks like the slippery slope to the afterlife, the one that brainless mummy guys are always trying to find.

"There is no time to argue," Mr. Klopper gasps, grabbing a torch off the wall next to the entrance to the tomb. "Here, take this," he says, shoving the torch into my hand and almost burning off my eyebrows.

"OUCH!" I scream. I gently touch my face to see if it feels like a cheese pizza. "Do I still have eyelashes?"

"We should have brought marshmallows," Hailey says, smacking me on the shoulder.

"Please keep your voices down," Mr. Klopper says, looking nervously down the hallway in both directions.

I flinch in alarm as my pants begin to squeal and oink as if I'm sitting on a hog the size of a blimp.

This dang Farmer Fred phone is going to put me in prison!

"Wow! I didn't know there was a pig in the rotation!" Hailey laughs. "That is so cool."

Despite all these distractions, I'm still worried that the suspiciously empty animal crackers box will be uncovered as the way Mr. Klopper smuggled the mummy head in and out of the museum. I hand him the box. "Hide this where Benito won't find it," I say. "We need to buy as much time as possible."

"Where?" he asks, taking the box like it's a ticking bomb.

"Leave it on the sidewalk outside the back door we came through," Hailey suggests.

"They might think it's related to the scarab being used as a doorstop."

"Good idea," I say. The giant pig snorts again from my pocket. "And just deny that you had anything to do with anything until you hear from me."

"Quick, they're coming!" Mr. Klopper says, and pushes me toward the stairs. Just as the enormous pig in my pants squeals for a third time, I swallow the lump in my throat, hold the torch out in front of me, and scurry down the stairs.

"This is amazing," Hailey whispers just inches from my ear. "They wouldn't let us come down here on our Minds of Tomorrow tour. This is strictly for members only."

"Then we need to fill out an application," I whisper back, as we continue deeper and deeper into what looks like an actual Egyptian tomb.

As earsplitting pig sounds echo off the walls of the cramped stairwell, I can't help but think that my mom is more popular than I ever imagined. Finally the oinking stops. Several seconds later the cell phone whinnies like a horse.

"Somebody's left a message," says Hailey.

"I can't wait to hear the donkey," I grumble.

We reach the bottom of the stairs and step slowly into some sort of underground chamber. I feel sand under my feet. I smell dead things. I wonder if mummy tombs come equipped with bathrooms.

Hailey clears her throat. "Uh, I'm not so sure a donkey can be classified as a classic farm animal."

"WHAT ABOUT THAT?" I wail, thrusting the torch into the air to protect us from an enormous monster emerging from the darkness. It has the body of a giant man and the face of a snarling and hungry-looking dog!

And dogs have never liked me!

· Chapter Sixteen ·
Monster Terror

"RUN FOR YOUR LIFE!"

"Have you lost your mind?" Hailey growls from behind me.

"NO! There's some kind of monster-dog-man thing coming this way!" I screech.

"That's just Anubis, you nutcase," Hailey says, grabbing the torch out of my hand and walking over to the giant. "See?" she says, slapping the monster on the shin. "It's just a statue. He's the god of the dead and the guardian of tombs and stuff. Egyptian priests often wore a mask like this one during mummy-making rituals."

"Neat," I croak, blinking into the darkness. "In the flickering light of the torch I thought it was—"

"Don't worry," she says, "I won't tell anybody." She hands the torch back to me. "And that's not a dog, it's a jackal."

"I was just thinking that," I say in a not-very-convincing way.

"A jackal is sort of like a coyote, hyena, and fox all rolled into one," she says. "But don't worry, they don't live around here," she adds. She walks over to a mummy-shaped golden coffin near the back of the tomb.

As you may remember, I'm not the most comfortable guy in the dark, so I'm thankful to have the torch. As Hailey oohs and aahs

over the sparkly mummy box, I finally have a peaceful moment to organize my thoughts.

I've had this nagging, tugging feeling that I'm missing something. It's as if the answer I'm seeking is right out in front of me, just beyond the tip of my tongue.

Everything I've learned so far feels like it's been dropped into a blender and whipped into a frenzy. So I take a moment to put everything in order, like a mental shopping list—from the animal crackers box and the head of lettuce to the scribbled note and the other museum directors visiting today. I scan my third eye up and down my imaginary list, waiting for something to jump out at me and sock me in the recently fried eye.

It's as if I'm in a trance. In fact, I may be drooling, but I can't be sure.

A dozen puzzle pieces that have been swirling around in my head suddenly start to arrange themselves, like ducks in a row. Then they start clicking in a line, like dominoes falling one after the next. It's a feeling that's hard to describe—sort of like a rose blossoming between your ears or the surprise of stepping in fresh dog poop in your bare feet.

"I've done it again," I say quietly to myself.

Pulling solutions to baffling mysteries out of thin air is my specialty, but I surprise even myself sometimes.

While Hailey is distracted by the golden coffin, I pull out the cell phone, snap it open, and hit the telephone number that I hope will save Mr. Klopper and my fourth case as a private detective from ruin.

It may be a long shot, but it's the only shot we've got.

small fire + **cupcakes** + **dancing goat**

A COMPLICATED PLAN

I may have solved the mystery, but it might be too late.

I'm not so sure I can still get everything to fall into place in time to save Mr. Klopper from disaster.

I spend several tense minutes pacing around, mumbling to myself. I work out a complicated plan in my head that involves a small fire, a large box of cupcakes, and a dancing goat. But will it work?

Hailey is saying something to me, but I can't hear her. I'm so lost in my own thoughts, I haven't even had a chance to tell her what's happened.

Before I can even open my mouth, Hailey pulls the torch from my hand and rolls it in the sand, extinguishing the only light in the tomb. I once again have the wool pulled over my eyes!

"Why did you—" I begin to hiss, but Hailey pushes my chin around so I can see a pair of mummy's legs coming down the stairs.

They say seeing is believing, but I think my eyes are lying! "How could—"

Hailey pulls me behind the golden coffin. Has the headless mummy somehow come to life? Is it hunting us? Can it still eat us if its stomach was dropped into a jar a few thousand years ago?

I peer over the top of the coffin and clearly make out the mummy's feet and knees in what appears to be light from a torch. The mummy seems to be hesitating. Maybe negotiating stairs without your head is trickier than any of us can imagine!

I hold my breath as the rest of the mummy emerges from the stairwell. With a wave of relief, I see that this mummy has a head!

And it's wearing glasses?

What the. . . ? I consider asking Hailey if the Egyptians invented corrective eyewear, but then I see some of the stuffing spilling out of the mummy's chest. Disgusting!

"Sherlock Sherlock?" the mummy calls out, holding up its torch.

That's not stuffing! It's beard! Why in the name of Anubis is Mr. Klopper dressed as a mummy?

Mr. Klopper seems to notice our confusion. "The people serving drinks to the arriving guests upstairs are wearing this costume," he explains. "It's a museum tradition. So I just borrowed this as a disguise."

"That's the worst disguise I've ever seen," Hailey says. "You're wearing big nerd glasses and you've got beard poking out all over the place."

"And I think it's giving me a horrible rash," Mr. Klopper says in agreement, moaning

slightly as he scratches his thigh. "We're almost out of time."

"I've solved the mystery," I announce abruptly.

"YOU HAVE?" they both cry out in surprise. The sound echoes off the chamber walls.

"Quiet," I shush them as I start up the stairs. Mr. Klopper's unexpected arrival has convinced me to throw out my previous plan. Besides, I'm not sure I can get my hands on a large box of cupcakes, anyway. In its place, I have instantly cooked up an even better, but riskier, plan.

"But how—" Hailey begins.

"No time for questions! Follow me! We haven't a moment to lose!"

I almost sound like The Great Detective himself, except for the squeeze of fear you can hear in my throat.

• Chapter Eighteen •
Of Mice and Men

My dad always says that things aren't over till the fat lady sings.

I have no idea what that means.

But I'm about ready for a big lady to take the stage and get the show started.

The next several minutes are a blur of hallways, stairways, and wrong ways. I'm reminded of laboratory mice running around in a maze. Or should I say three blind mice?

Because not only do I not know where I'm going, I'm determined to get there fast. Add in the fact that we're being followed by a mob led by Benito the snarling security guard, and you have a recipe for disaster.

I have to keep stopping to wait for Hailey and Mr. Klopper, who's leaving a trail of mummy wrappings behind him that would make Hansel and Gretel proud.

Finally, I turn into the hallway with the locking broom closet and crash through the emergency exit.

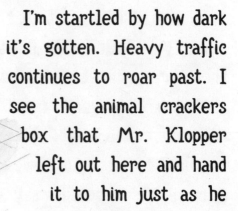

I'm startled by how dark it's gotten. Heavy traffic continues to roar past. I see the animal crackers box that Mr. Klopper left out here and hand it to him just as he comes wheezing through the door.

"But Sherlock Sherlock," he gasps, looking at the box like it's a hot potato that he'd rather not handle again. "I thought you wanted me to hide this from Benito."

"Now I want you to take it inside and say you've saved the museum from a terrible embarrassment," I say, grabbing the door before it closes again.

"I don't—"

"The mummy's head is in the box!" I

practically scream, motioning him toward the door. "Now, go in there and tell them that you've saved the day. You've found the head that they haven't even realized has been stolen yet. I'm sure you can do that."

Mr. Klopper looks as though he's seen a ghost. He slowly opens the box and looks inside. He blinks several times. "How did you . . ."

"It doesn't really matter now, does it?" I say, pushing Mr. Klopper back through the door.

As if she can't believe what she's hearing, Hailey stops Mr. Klopper and looks inside. "Gross," she says quietly.

I gently push her aside. And shut the door on Mr. Klopper.

"Can you hear that?" I ask Hailey.

"What?" she asks.

"That's the sound of the fat lady singing."

"Okay, what just happened?" Hailey asks, standing in front of me with her fists on her hips.

"A magician never reveals his secrets," I say with a laugh. This whole ordeal was worth it just to see her so confused and mixed up.

Not long after the door closed behind Mr. Klopper, I used my mom's cell phone to call our house. She's on her way to pick us up. I told her to hurry. So now I'm watching the oncoming traffic to flag her down when she approaches.

"Oh, yeah?" Hailey says, giving me a look that only a little sister can. "How about if I call Sharon Sheldon and tell her you love her? Or should I tell Irene Adler that you want to be her boyfriend? Or maybe I should tell Mom you murdered Doreen with your big, fat butt?"

"Take it easy!" I wail. "Don't go wacko on me."

"All's fair in love and war," she says.

"It's simple, really," I say. "I don't know why I didn't see it earlier.

"Look, the lettuce and the note were always the things that didn't fit."

"Yes, that was weird," Hailey agrees.

"And the little note had 'butt' written on it."

"Yeah, so?"

"Well, it occurred to me that *b-u-t-t* is the beginning of 'butter.' As in butter lettuce. As in the thing Mr. Klopper found in the box."

"And so?" Hailey asks, shaking her head.

"And so, the note was probably cut out of a packet of butter lettuce seeds," I tell her.

"Keep talking," she says, waving her hands impatiently.

"When we were at the Kloppers' house, Mrs. Klopper asked you to have tea in the garden while I went down into the basement. I pictured a garden with flowers and fountains, but it was actually a vegetable garden, wasn't it?"

"Yes, it was," she says. "But are you saying Mr. Klopper stole his own head?"

"No, Mrs. Klopper did!" I say. Hailey remains silent, thinking. "She was mad at him for forgetting about their anniversary. So she took the head as a prank, a trick. That's why the note made no sense. She probably just copied a few symbols out of one of his books."

"Would she really do that?" Hailey asks, shocked at the thought.

"She told me she did it!" I say. "I called her when we were down in the tomb. She didn't know the head was going to be needed for tonight's party. Remember, she doesn't like

to hear about his museum work anymore. She was just doing it to get back at him. To teach him a lesson. A simple joke gone horribly wrong. She felt terrible that he was in danger of losing his job or getting arrested. So I asked her to drive it over here and put it in the animal crackers box outside the back door."

"That's something," Hailey whispers.

We both step back as Mom honks and pulls the car to the curb in front of us.

"Did you pee your pants, Sherlock? I'm so sorry, sweetie. I got here as fast as I could!"

"Mom, he's got serious bladder issues," Hailey says through the window.

I roll my eyes. "I told Mrs. Klopper to keep the whole thing to herself, to not mention anything about it," I say to Hailey before I open the car's back door. "It's better that way for everyone involved. That includes you."

"Or what?" Hailey snips. "Are you gonna sit

on me till I pop, too? Haven't you killed enough sisters for one day?" She finally grows tired of waiting for me to open the door and she looks me in the eyes. "Okay already! My lips are zipped, brother big butt."

I believe her.

As we climb into the backseat of my mom's car, I'm struck by the fact that I've done it again. I've solved my fourth case as a private detective.

But there will be no stories about this in the *Baskerville Daily News*. No certificate of thanks from the museum. And no bragging around the dinner table. This is the kind of case that's better left a secret.

But that's okay with me.

Every case closed brings me one step closer to life as a detective and gives me a little more proof that I was born with a gift.